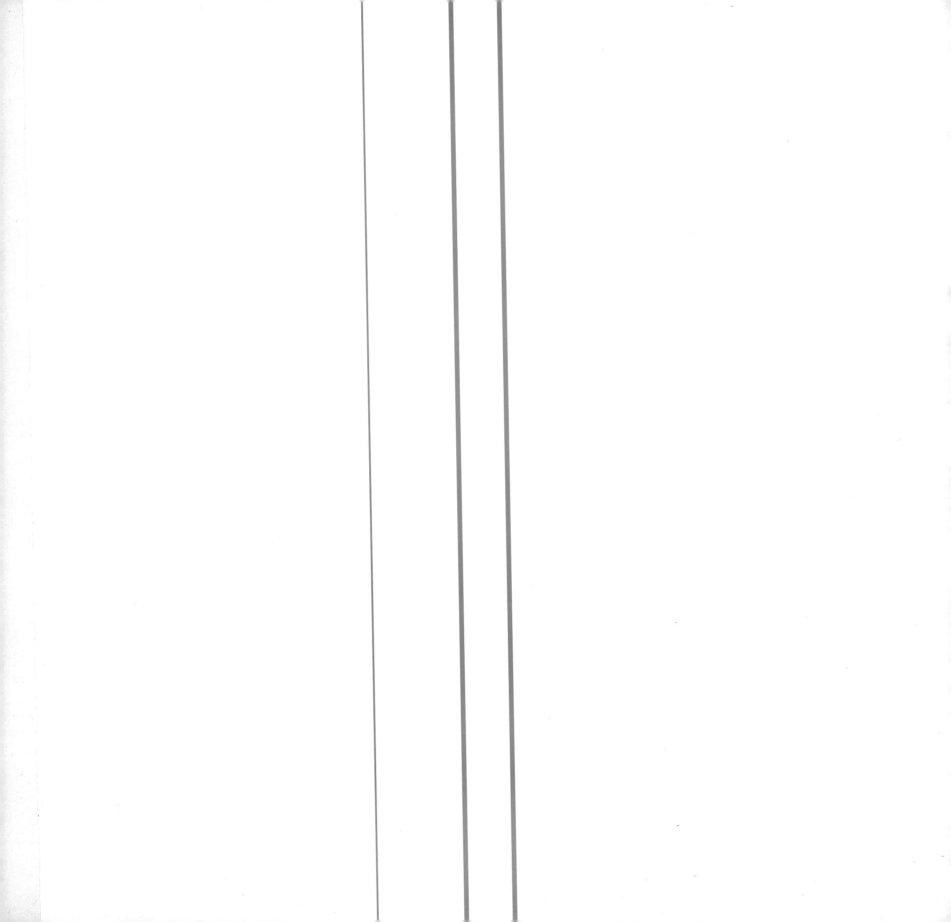

For Kit and Arthur who saw the seal and
heard the music, and for the children of
Harold Magnay School, Liverpool
for their inspiration.

Seal
Surfer

MICHAEL FOREMAN

Andersen Press • London

SPRING

One day in early spring an old man and his grandson climbed carefully down to a rocky beach. They were looking for mussels.

As the boy searched he noticed a slight movement among the rocks. Then he saw the seal. It was difficult to see her body against the rocks, except for a smudge of red on her belly.

"Look, Grandad," cried the boy. "The seal is injured."

"Best not to go too close," said Grandad, and they watched the seal from a distance.

The seal looked quite calm, lying still in the morning sun, and after a while the boy started hunting for mussels again.

When he next looked up at the seal, instead of a smudge of red he saw a flash of white. A seal pup, snow white and just born, was nuzzling its mother.

"Quick, Grandad," whispered the boy. "Let's get some fish for the seals."

As the spring days lengthened the man and the boy often watched the seal family. The pup's white coat moulted and she became the colour of the rocks. She often moved to the water's edge to watch her mother fish. She also saw the boy and the old man watching from the clifftop as she basked in the warm sun.

SUMMER

Then one day in early summer the boy watched as the mother seal pushed her pup off the rocks and into the sea. The shock of the cold water made the young seal panic. The water closed over her head. She pushed upwards with her tail and flippers until her head burst through to the surface.

Now her mother dived into the water and together they swam round and round — diving down, twisting and turning and corkscrewing into the depths. As the seal pup burst back up through the surface of the water, she saw the boy cheer.

AUTUMN

The boy did not see the seals again until the summer days were fading. One evening in early autumn, he went down to the harbour to meet his grandad returning from a day's fishing. He saw Grandad's old pick-up truck with the door open. The radio was on and the music of Beethoven filled the air.

Grandad was staring into the water. The whiskery face of the mother seal stared back at him like a reflection in the moonlit mirror of the harbour.

Grandad tossed the seal a fish — and another. The boy watched as the mirror dissolved and then reformed and dissolved again as they all shared the fish and the music of Beethoven.

WINTER

While the wet winter winds buffeted the boy on his way to school, the young seal learned the lessons of the sea.

She often swam alone far from home, exploring the coast. She loved the days of great rolling waves, when the sea brimmed and shimmered with fish. She learned to fish by swimming deep and looking up to see the fish outlined against the sky.

She learned to sleep at sea, floating upright like a bottle, with just her nose above the surface. But best of all she loved to haul herself up onto rocks with other young seals to feel the sun and the wind on her skin.

But one day the wind rose suddenly into a full-blown gale. Rain and mountainous waves wrenched great rocks from the cliffs. The young seals dived to try to escape the falling boulders. But even in the sea they were in danger and some were dashed against the rocks and crushed.

SPRING

The warmth of spring brought wild flowers and the boy and his grandad to the cliffs once more. But there was no sign of the young seal.

The mother seal still came to the harbour for an evening of fish and music .

"The young seal must have died in the winter storms," said the boy.

SUMMER

As spring warmed into summer the boy went each Saturday to the Surf School. He was a strong swimmer and after much practice he was ready to go 'outback' with the other surfers.

One sunny day, he lay on his board as it rose and fell on the gently rocking swell. Suddenly he was aware of a different movement in the water. A dark shape swooped under the board and spiralled down and back up. The gleaming face of the young seal popped up beside his own.

The sea was gathering itself for some bigger waves. The boy could see the dark green walls of water lining up on the horizon. The seal could sense the movement in the water. They let the first two waves pass, then together they rode the third huge rolling wave towards the shore.

All afternoon, side by side, the boy and the seal surfed together. Then quite suddenly the seal was gone. The boy watched for a while and then let the next good wave carry him all the way to the beach.

The next day, at just that same perfect state of the tide, the young seal was back. Again the boy and the seal began to surf together.

The boy could not take his eyes off the seal as she flashed through the water. As he concentrated on watching her, the wave he was riding broke suddenly and plunged him headfirst from his board. He somersaulted, churning over and over. He struck a rock and the water, thick with sand, filled his nose and mouth. He was being pushed deeper and deeper. He was falling into darkness.

Then he felt a different sensation. His body was being forced upwards. He could see the sunlight through the water and feel the seal under his body, pushing. With a final heave the seal flipped him onto his board. He clung on, and the next wave carried him to the shore. His friends crowded round to make sure he was all right. Once he had got his breath back the boy felt fine.

The following afternoon, and for all the long, hot summer, the boy surfed with the seal.

WINTER

The wonderful summer was followed by the worst of winters.
The storms smashed the rocks and churned up the sand and stones.
The beach was deserted. No seal came there now.

SPRING

When spring next brought the wild flowers to the cliffs, it brought the boy but not his grandfather. The boy and his friends ventured far along the cliffs but they could find no sign of seals.

SUMMER

As the evenings grew lighter towards summer the boy took to fishing from the quay, as his grandad had done before. One evening, as he watched the still water, two shiny heads broke the surface. The boy cheered as he saw it was the once young seal, now as whiskery as Grandad, and with her a young pup.

The boy smiled. He knew then that he would ride the waves with the seals throughout that summer and every summer.

And maybe one day he would lie on the clifftops with his own grandchildren and together they would watch the seals.